Richard Scarry's
HILDA NEEDS HELP!

A GOLDEN BOOK • NEW YORK

Western Publishing Company, Inc., Racine, Wisconsin 53404

The Cat family and Lowly Worm are going on a vacation to the seaside. It is a long trip. They will sleep on the train. A taxi drives them to the station.

On the station platform they see Hilda Hippo.
She is crying.

"What is the matter, Hilda?" Father Cat asks.

"I can't find my train ticket!" Hilda wails.
"Without it, the conductor won't let me on board.
"My vacation is ruined!"

Huckle sees a small piece of paper next to Hilda's foot. "Isn't THIS your ticket?" Huckle asks, holding it up.

"Oh, thank you, Huckle!" Hilda says. "It must have fallen out of my purse."

The conductor shows Hilda her compartment. "Here is the light, here is the sink, and here is the alarm," he says. "But don't touch the alarm unless there is an emergency."

Then the conductor shows the Cat family their compartment. Huckle and Lowly choose the top berth. The stationmaster gives the signal to go, and the train pulls out of Busytown station.

A bell rings
in the corridor.

The conductor announces that dinner is being served in the dining car. The Cat family walks to the dining car and sits down at a table.

"AAAHHH!" There is a scream outside the door of the dining car. Hilda Hippo has been shut between two coaches. The conductor rushes to the door and lets Hilda in. She sits down at a table.

"It's fun to eat while watching the countryside zoom by!" says Huckle.

The waiter tries to balance a bowl of soup from the kitchen.

SPLASH! The soup lands on Hilda's dress.
"AAAHHH!" Hilda screams. "My dress is ruined!"
Crying, she runs back to her compartment.

When the Cat family has finished dinner, they return to their compartment. They see Hilda Hippo crying in the corridor.

"What is the matter now?" Father Cat asks.
"It is so terrible!" screams Hilda. "There's a
man in my room!"

Father Cat reaches for the door. Out steps the
conductor. "Your berth is ready for the night, Miss
Hippo!" he says.

The Cat family gets ready for bed. They all brush their teeth in the little sink.

"What an exciting trip!" says Father Cat, switching off the light.

"AAAGGGHHHH!!!"
The Cat family hears a familiar scream.
SCREECH! goes the train.
BUMP! THUMP! go the Cat family suitcases, tumbling to the floor. The train has come to a stop.

The conductor, the engineer, and Father Cat run
to Hilda's compartment to see what the trouble is.
"It's terrible!" Hilda cries. "Someone help me! My
earring has fallen down the drain!"

The conductor looks down the drain.

He tries to reach the earring, but the drain is too narrow.

Then the engineer tries to pull it out with his screwdriver, but that doesn't work, either.

Lowly and Huckle come to watch.
"Father Cat," says Lowly, "I have an
idea." He whispers something in his ear.

Then Lowly stands on the rim of
the sink. Father Cat holds Lowly's hat.
Huckle holds on to Lowly's foot.

Lowly takes a deep breath and dives into the drainpipe.

Soon he signals Huckle with a wiggle of his foot. Huckle pulls him out. POP!

Hilda Hippo's shiny earring is in Lowly's mouth.
"Bravo, Lowly! Bravo, Huckle!" she says.
She gives Lowly a big hug.
Everyone says good night.

The train rolls on, undisturbed, to the seaside.
Hilda has a wonderful vacation.
So does the Cat family!